Addy's Race

ORCA
YOUNG
READERS

Addy's Race

DEBBY WALDMAN

ORCA BOOK PUBLISHERS

Library and Archives Canada Cataloguing in Publication

Waldman, Debby
Addy's race / Debby Waldman.
(Orca young readers)

Issued also in electronic formats.
ISBN 978-1-55469-924-7

I. Title. II. Series: Orca young readers
PS8645.A457A64 2011   JC813'.6   C2011-903480-8

First published in the United States, 2011
Library of Congress Control Number: 2011929399

Summary: Addy joins her school's running club and learns not only is she a great runner,
but she can also be assertive and let others know there is more to her than hearing loss.

*Orca Book Publishers is dedicated to preserving the environment and has printed this book
on paper certified by the Forest Stewardship Council®.*

Orca Book Publishers gratefully acknowledges the support for its publishing programs
provided by the following agencies: the Government of Canada through the
Canada Book Fund and the Canada Council for the Arts, and the Province of
British Columbia through the BC Arts Council and the Book Publishing Tax Credit.

Cover artwork by Alana McCarthy

ORCA BOOK PUBLISHERS
PO Box 5626, Stn. B
Victoria, BC Canada
V8R 6S4

ORCA BOOK PUBLISHERS
PO Box 468
Custer, WA USA
98240-0468

www.orcabook.com
Printed and bound in Canada.

14 13 12 11 • 4 3 2 1

For Elizabeth and Noah

Chapter 1

You would not believe how many people expect me to be like Helen Keller. Not the blind part—it's obvious I'm not blind. I'm not banging into walls or carrying a cane or being led by a dog wearing a harness. I don't even need glasses.

And it's obvious I can talk. As soon as anyone asks, "Don't you speak sign language?" (usually while waving their hands around as if *they're* speaking sign language), I say, "I don't have to. I'm not deaf. I hear fine with my hearing aids."

Then they act surprised. The ones who watch the Discovery Channel ask, "Why don't you have those bionic things for your ears?" They're talking about cochlear implants. I want to say, "Are *you* the one with the hearing problem? Cochlear implants are for deaf people. I just told you I hear fine with my hearing aids."

When I say that—minus the first sentence—they act disappointed, as if I said there's no such thing as Santa or the Tooth Fairy. As if it would be better if I couldn't hear at all.

The people who feel sorry for me are worse. It's not as if I'm dying of cancer or can't walk or have flippers for arms. I can't hear as well as most people, that's all.

Last week an old woman in the grocery store looked at my hearing aids and said, "Oh, you poor dear! It must be so difficult for you." I wanted to say, *Wait till you get hearing aids. It's going to be a lot more difficult for you—you'll have to get used to them. I've been wearing them my whole life.*

But instead I put on my sweet Addy face and said, "Thank you." I don't think my mother even heard the old woman talking to me. Which is a good thing. If she had, she would have launched into her "How I Found Out about Addy's Hearing Loss and What a Tragedy It Was for Me" story, in which she is the heroine with a handicapped child and my role is to generate pity for her.

My mother was an actress before she married my father. She was in commercials for dishwashing soap, laundry detergent, canned soup and salad dressings. She says making the ads prepared her to be a stay-at-home mom.

I think she misses being in front of the camera. When she talks about how she found out about my hearing loss, she gets very dramatic. This is how she starts her story: "When we brought Addy home from the hospital, Rick (that's my dad) rang a bell next to her ear. When she didn't turn her head, he said, 'I don't think she can hear,' and I said, 'Rick, she's four days old. No four-day-old baby can turn her head!'"

If my father is nearby, he smiles as if he's thinking, There she goes again. I roll my eyes. My mother never notices.

The second part of her story goes like this: "When Addy got a little older, Rick got upset because she didn't greet him at the door. I said, 'Rick, she's not like the dogs you grew up with. She's not going to run to the door with your slippers and the newspaper as soon as you come home.'"

I don't know what she's talking about. Even on television, I've never seen a dog run to a door with slippers and a newspaper. The dogs I know eat slippers and pee on newspapers.

The third part of my mother's story makes me the maddest: "When Addy was a year and a half, Rick came home from a business trip and all he could talk about was how the baby next to him could make animal noises. As if somehow I had failed as a parent because I hadn't taught our daughter to moo, bark and oink."

This is where I want to say, *No, Mom. I failed. Me. Addy. Not you*. But it's her story. Fortunately I can turn off my hearing aids, so I don't have to listen.

"You are so lucky," my best friend Lucy says when she picks me up on the first day of school. "I wish I could turn off my mother."

"What did she do this time?"

"She told Miss Fielding I'm joining running club. I hate running. She knows that."

I feel bad for Lucy. Her mother, Joanne, is a jock. She runs about ten miles a day, more if she's training for a marathon, triathlon or biathlon—any kind of "on" that involves sweating and a finish line.

She's trying to make Lucy into a jock, but Lucy doesn't even like gym. She's the biggest girl in our school. She's as tall as some of the teachers, and she's not even twelve. My mother says she's solid, "like a farmer's wife." She said that to my aunt on the phone when she thought nobody was listening.

Lucy thinks she takes after her father. I've seen pictures of him. He does kind of look like a farmer. He died of a heart attack when Lucy was four.

Joanne says there's nothing wrong with Lucy's heart, it's just that she doesn't want to try. That's not true. Lucy will try anything, but why should she join a club she's not interested in? One thing about Joanne though—she's stubborn. So Lucy is stuck in running club.

"I'll do it with you," I said.

"Really?"

I nodded, wishing I could take it back. Running makes me sweat, and sweat makes my hearing aids slimy. Plus, I'm not very fast. Then again, neither is Lucy.

Chapter 2

"You know who's going to be in running club this year?" Lucy said.

Before I could guess, Stephanie and Emma appeared on either side of us. Stephanie looked at Lucy and said, "Hey, my mom says you're joining running club."

She was acting so friendly, if you didn't know better, you'd think she was nice. But Stephanie and Emma are never nice. They think they're better than everybody. And because they dress alike and wear their hair the same way and spend all their time together, they're like one person in two bodies, which means they take up twice as much space, like some kind of superhero, but not the good kind.

I think of them as Stem. Like part of a plant. A stink-weed plant.

They always behave around teachers, so teachers love them. If you get stuck doing a project with them, they'll suck up to you until you end up doing the work, which frees them to brush their hair, compare notes about what their mothers bought them at Aritzia and lululemon, and flirt with boys.

They were the most irritating people in grade five. Also grades four, three, two, one and kindergarten. The first day of school hadn't officially started yet, and already it looked as if they were going to win the award again for grade six.

"You're not even good in gym," Emma said. "Why would you want to be in running club?"

Emma had what my grandmother would call diarrhea of the mouth—no control over what came out, no matter how unpleasant. "Why do you care?" I said.

"I'm not talking to you." Emma looked at my hearing aids. "I guess you couldn't tell."

"Excuse me?" I said. Was she trying to make a joke? Or had the summer turned her from stupid and annoying to just plain mean?

Emma flipped her hair back. "I said, I guess you couldn't hear. And obviously you couldn't." She looked at Stephanie and gave her a high five. Stephanie looked surprised, as if she couldn't believe what she'd heard either. But she high-fived her back. I wanted to high-five both of them. Across the face. Lucy pulled me away before I had a chance.

"I can't believe her," Lucy said as we hurried down the block.

"It's okay," I said, although it wasn't. Whenever anyone says something mean or stupid, my grandmother says, sticks and stones may break your bones but names will never hurt you. My mother says, consider the source. I don't know why grown-ups think cute sayings make things hurt less.

Lucy stopped at the corner. "I wish we went to a different school."

"I wish they did," I said. "In a different country. Or a different solar system."

"It's all Stephanie's fault I have to be in running club," Lucy said.

"What do you mean?"

"The only reason my mother knows there is a running club is because we bumped into Stephanie's mom at Safeway last week and she said Stephanie was joining."

Stephanie's mother, Sandy, is friends with Joanne. Lucy and Stephanie have known each other their whole lives, longer than I've known Lucy. But they stopped being friends the first day of kindergarten, when Stephanie discovered Emma.

"My mother said, 'Isn't that wonderful! Lucy's joining running club too!'" Lucy shook her head. "I was like, 'I am? I don't want to be in running club,' and she said, 'Of course you do,' and Sandy said, 'You'll have such fun with Stephanie.'"

We were at the edge of the schoolyard. My favorite thing about the first day is watching the kindergartners. Some of them are excited, but most cling to their parents like barnacles to a rock. On my first day of kindergarten, I was a barnacle. So was Lucy. Our mothers stayed that whole morning. Emma and Stephanie's mothers disappeared right away, but Stem didn't care. They were drawn to each other like magnets. My grandmother would say they're like two peas in a pod. I hate peas.

"Do you remember in kindergarten when we were playing kickball and Emma fell and blamed it on me?" I asked Lucy.

Lucy nodded. "She said it was because you were in the way and didn't hear her coming. But it was because she tripped over her shoelace. Hey, what are those two doing?"

She was looking toward the playground at Miranda and Kelsey, who are twins but don't even look related. Miranda's hair is the color of Becel margarine, and she has so many freckles that from a distance her skin looks brown. Kelsey, who comes up to Miranda's shoulders, has dark hair and plain skin.

They were crouched in a circle with a bunch of kids, looking at something. "They're shells from the Great Barrier Reef," Miranda said when we got closer.

"Our uncle lives in Australia," Kelsey added, moving over so we could see. There were dozens of shells, all different shapes and sizes. "We went last month."

"It's illegal to take stuff from the Great Barrier Reef," said a nerdy-looking boy I didn't know.

Kelsey looked insulted. "They're from the beach, not the reef." She held out a curved shell almost as big as my fist. "Put it up to your ear and listen. It's really cool."

Lucy took it. "Wow. That's amazing." She handed it to me. "It's all whooshy."

I put it up against my hearing aid. All I could hear was the crunchy sound of shell against plastic.

"Isn't it cool?" Lucy asked.

I shook my head. "I didn't hear anything." I tried not to sound mad. It wasn't her fault.

"Maybe if you take off your hearing aid?" Lucy suggested. "And go somewhere quiet?"

I shook my head. Some things I will never hear.

Chapter 3

Lucy kept apologizing. "It's okay. Stop already," I said. We were hanging our backpacks in our cubbies at the back of the grade six room. Everyone looked at us to see who was talking so loudly.

I could feel my face turning the same color as Emma's red lululemon hoodie. Stephanie, who says her hair is strawberry blond even though it's orange, was wearing a green one. The combination of her hair and the hoodie made her look like a life-sized bag of frozen peas and carrots.

Beside her sat a new girl who was busy tying her plaid high-tops. She wasn't paying attention to anyone. She looked like a GapKids model with perfect hair: long, straight and so blond it was white.

I walked to the front of the room to give Mrs. Shewchuk my FM transmitter. She wears it around her neck, like a necklace. Whatever she says goes from the transmitter microphone straight into my ears. I hate it, but my mother says I have to use it; otherwise I might not hear everything my teacher says. What she doesn't realize is that I don't always *want* to.

In grade two, the substitute forgot to turn off the FM when she was helping Stephanie write in her journal. Stephanie asked how to spell *cooties* because that girl over there—she pointed at me—had them.

The sub said there was no such thing as cooties. Stephanie said, "Then I'll just write she smells bad." I turned off my hearing aids, so I never heard if the substitute told her there was no such thing as smelling bad.

At least with hearing aids, if my hair is loose, nobody can tell there's anything wrong with me. But the FM is like a billboard that says, *I'm a freak.* On my first day of kindergarten, Mrs. Ferris stood in front of the class and looked at me, tapped on the transmitter and said, "Addy? Addy? Come in, Addy. Can you hear me?" As if I were in outer space and she was at Cape Canaveral.

Of course I could hear her. Everyone could. But I was so embarrassed I couldn't answer. Finally Mom got out of her chair at the back of the room and took the FM into the hall to check it. She made me go with her. That was even more embarrassing.

At recess, Mom told Mrs. Ferris it wasn't a good idea to tap on the transmitter and single me out. But by then it was too late. The class was convinced I was part robot. It wasn't until a few days later, when Trevor Finney peed his pants during story time, that people stopped thinking I was so interesting.

Because it was the first day of school, Mrs. Shewchuk hadn't made a seating chart. I sat up front anyway, beside Lucy. The new girl took the desk on the other side of Lucy. Her posture was perfect, as if she had a board against her back.

I surveyed the room. Kelsey and Miranda were next to each other, arranging their supplies in their desks. Behind them, Trevor Finney, wearing a T-shirt with mud stains down the front, chewed his pencil and jiggled his legs.

Next to Trevor sat a new boy with curly dark hair and a Bench T-shirt. It was almost the same color blue as his eyes. Behind him was the nerdy-looking boy who had been checking out Miranda and Kelsey's shells. He needed a haircut.

When I turned to the front again, I noticed Mrs. Shewchuk was wearing a boom mic attached to a headband. It looked like the kind of mic Lady Gaga and Madonna wear in videos. A second FM transmitter hung around her neck.

Boom mics are for people with really bad hearing. Someone in my class was more deaf than me.

Was it the nerdy boy? He was in the row behind me, on the other side of the room. His hair covered his ears, so I couldn't tell for sure. When he saw me staring, his face brightened into a big, dopey smile.

Yuck. *I do not like you!* I yelled inside my head. He didn't get the message and kept smiling.

"Class!" Mrs. Shewchuk clapped her hands to get our attention. She stood by the SMART Board and beamed at us. "Welcome to grade six. We have three new students this year. Let's welcome them with a big Mackenzie School round of applause, shall we?"

She waited while we clapped. Then she looked at the new girl. "Sierra, why don't you say hello?" Straight-backed Sierra waved as if she were on a float in the end-of-the-day parade at Disneyland.

"And over here we have Henry, who comes to us from"—Mrs. Shewchuk looked at her desk briefly—"Calgary." The nerdy boy stood and waved. No one waved back. He winked at me. I looked at my desk, hoping no one had noticed.

"And behind Henry is Tyler, who comes to us from Black Diamond." The Bench T-shirt boy stood and bowed, a big, exaggerated gesture. Some kids laughed. Tyler didn't seem to notice. Was he the deaf kid? It was hard to tell—his curly hair sprung out everywhere and covered his ears too.

Who was the deaf kid? Shouldn't Mrs. Shewchuk have told me last week, when Mom and I met with her to go over my program plan?

Sometime between writing out all the things she has to do to make me stand out in class—like putting me in the front row, repeating things to make sure I've heard them, and telling everyone not to shuffle their feet, flip through their books or whisper anywhere near me—she could have said, "Addy, you're not going to be the only hard of hearing child in Mackenzie School anymore. You're not even going to be the only hard of hearing child in our class! You'll have company! It will be…"

Who was it?

"Addy?" Mrs. Shewchuk was standing by my desk. How long had she been trying to get my attention? "Are your hearing aids on?"

I gulped. Some people giggled. I couldn't bring myself to see who. It was probably Emma, high-fiving Stephanie again.

The hearing aids were on, but the FM receivers weren't. Mrs. Shewchuk and Mom had said if I didn't keep the receivers on I'd have to stay inside for recess. Did this mean I had to miss recess? I'd forgotten, that was all. And not even on purpose.

"I'm sorry," I said. "What was the question?"

"I asked about your summer," she said.

I wanted to say, "I told you about it last week at my program meeting, right after my mother told you about my first hearing test when I was three years old. The one where she sat in the testing booth and cried because I wasn't responding to the beeps. Just like I'm going to cry if you make me stay inside for recess."

But instead I told Mrs. Shewchuk the highlight of my summer was a road trip to see my grandmother, and that we visited Head-Smashed-In Buffalo Jump, Yellowstone National Park and Mount Rushmore.

She moved on to Peter Connelly next. He sits behind me. When I turned to get a better look, Henry was smiling at me again, as if he felt sorry for me. Maybe Mrs. Shewchuk had told him he had to stay in for recess too, if he didn't turn on his receivers.

Chapter 4

By the time the recess bell rang, I'd forgotten about everybody's summer holidays except Stem's. And obviously Mrs. Shewchuk had forgotten about the deal she made with my mother, because she let me go out.

It figured Stephanie and Emma had been to a summer running camp at the University of Alberta and were training with the Tornadoes. At first I thought they said tomatoes, and I couldn't figure out why anyone would train with tomatoes.

Stephanie said it was the best running club in Edmonton, but she says that about everything she does. She has the best violin teacher, dance teacher and acting teacher. She was almost in a commercial for McDonald's when she was six because she was the best actress, but they wanted a kid with brown hair, not strawberry blond. But of course, her hair was the best strawberry blond.

Lucy and I headed for the door with Kelsey and Miranda on either side of us. "Do you think people believe Stephanie when she says everything she does is the best?" I asked as we stepped outside.

"Only people who don't know her well enough to know better," Kelsey said.

We leaned against the school, watching some grade four kids fight over a basketball. In the field beside the basketball court, the grade five and six boys played soccer. Tyler had the ball. He was fast.

"Hey, there's that new girl—Sierra," Miranda said, pointing to the steps by the back entrance. "Sierra, over here," she yelled. Sierra looked around, but not at us.

"She seems stuck-up," Kelsey said.

"I don't think she sees us," Miranda said. But Miranda is hard to miss. She's almost as tall as Lucy.

"Maybe she's looking for someone," Lucy suggested.

"Who would she be looking for?" Miranda said. "She doesn't know anyone." She waved her arms as if they were wings and she was about to fly away. "Sierra! Over here!" But now Sierra was looking toward the playground.

"How do you know she doesn't know anyone?" I said. "Maybe she has a brother or sister in a lower grade."

Miranda shrugged. "I was just guessing."

"Or maybe she didn't hear you," Lucy pointed out.

"How could she not hear me?" Miranda said. "I was yelling as loud as I could."

I pointed to my hearing aids.

"But she's not hard of hearing," Miranda said. "You are."

"I'm not the only one."

"What do you mean?" Kelsey asked me.

"Mrs. Shewchuck was wearing two FM transmitters and that boom mic around her head."

"I wondered about that," Miranda said. "The only time I've seen something like that is in a music video."

"My aunt has one," Lucy said. "For the phone, so she can talk and do other stuff at the same time."

"Why would Mrs. Shewchuck wear something for her phone in school?" Miranda asked.

"Who knows," Lucy said.

"How do you know it's a boom mic for someone with hearing aids?" Kelsey asked me.

She was right. I didn't. It hadn't occurred to me it could be something else.

"Who do you think has hearing aids?" Lucy said.

"One of the new kids," I said. "I think Henry."

"Why him?" Lucy asked.

"He looks like a nerd."

"What does that have to do with hearing aids?" Miranda said. "You wear hearing aids and you don't look like a nerd."

"Thanks," I said. "But he does. He reminds me of a kid from the audiologist's."

"I think it's her," Miranda said, nodding toward Sierra.

"Stuck-up Sierra?" Kelsey asked.

"I don't think she's stuck-up," Lucy said. "She just couldn't hear us." She looked at me. "You always say it's hard to hear when it's noisy."

"I was waving so hard my arms are sore!" Miranda insisted. "Even if she couldn't hear, she could have seen me."

"I think we should go be nice to her," Lucy said.

"Me too," I said.

"Okay, fine," Miranda and Kelsey said, but while we were talking, Sierra had disappeared. We didn't see her again until we were back in Mrs. Shewchuk's room. She was in her desk, hunched over her scribbler. That's when I saw it. The transmitter, a pale-gold disc that looked like a miniature steering wheel, stuck to her head behind her ear.

Lucy and I were hanging our coats. She noticed it at the same time I did. "What's that thing?"

"Shhhh!" I said.

"What's what?" Stephanie said.

"Nothing," I hissed.

"What is your problem?" Emma asked.

"Girls!" Mrs. Shewchuk said. "Stop chatting and sit."

I walked slowly to my desk, trying to check out the transmitter without being obvious about it.

The only person I'd ever met with an implant was an older boy who got one when he was twelve. He spoke at a conference my mother took me to. He was an odd choice as a speaker because he couldn't talk well enough for anyone to understand him. He hadn't learned to speak until after he'd gotten the implant.

I wondered how well Sierra spoke. Maybe she was quiet because she was embarrassed about her voice.

Her hearing was worse than mine. If you're so deaf you can't hear with hearing aids, you get an implant. You have to have an operation. The surgeon puts electrodes inside your head and that colored steering-wheel thing outside. Everything is attached with magnets. I wondered what it would be like to have a head full of magnets. Would the inside of your skull look like a refrigerator door?

Sierra caught me staring. I don't like it when people stare at my hearing aids, and here I was, doing the same thing to her. I reached up and pushed my hair back. *Look at me*, I wanted to say. *I have a hearing aid. Kind of like your implant.* I gave her a friendly smile, so she'd see we had something in common. But she looked down at her notebook, avoiding me. Kelsey was right. Sierra was stuck-up.

For the rest of the morning my mind tried to wander, but it was hopeless. Because of the FM, the only way to get the teacher's voice out of my head is to turn off the receivers. And I couldn't do that, because Mrs. Shewchuk was already watching me closely.

I was so curious about Sierra. I wanted to talk to Lucy, but I couldn't. That's another drawback to being hard of hearing—having to sit at the front of the class. Not only could I not get Mrs. Shewchuk out of my head, I also couldn't get out of her sight.

I counted the minutes until lunch. When we were at our cubbies, getting our lunch bags, I tried to see the steering-wheel thing again, but I was on the wrong side of Sierra. All I could see was hair.

Then, as if she'd seen me staring, she stood up and said, "What are you looking at?"

I had always thought "eyes in the back of your head" was another of my grandmother's expressions, but maybe Sierra actually did have eyes in the back of her head. I was so startled, I jumped and landed on Emma's foot.

"What's the matter with you?" Emma snapped. "You're crushing my foot! I have running club today!"

I wanted to say, *So do I*, but then she would say, *You're not on the Tornadoes. Running isn't important for you!*

Arguing with a bad-tempered person is like throwing gasoline on a fire—another of my grandmother's sayings. So is "kill 'em with kindness."

I didn't want to kill Emma, but wounding her would be fun.

"I'm sorry," I said. "I'm clumsy."

Emma looked like a fish, her mouth open with no sound coming out. It was as if the message that the fight was over and she could stop yelling had gotten stuck between her brain and her voice. But if Emma said something else, I never heard, because Lucy was at the door and I had to follow her.

Miranda and Kelsey caught up with us. "Can we eat with you?" Kelsey asked. Last year she and Miranda ate with their older sister Jackie. But Jackie was in junior high now.

I looked at Lucy. "Sure," she said.

"Did you see that thing stuck to Sierra's head?" Miranda said.

"It's a cochlear implant," I said.

"Isn't that for deaf people?"

I nodded.

"She's deaf?" Miranda asked.

"I guess," I said.

"Where do you eat lunch?" Kelsey interrupted.

I pointed to a clearing at the edge of the soccer field. "Over there."

"We used to eat near the condos," Kelsey said.

"Kelsey, can you stop talking for a minute?" Miranda asked. She turned to me. "I thought there were special schools for deaf people. Why isn't she in a special school?"

How was I supposed to know? Miranda played violin. Did that make her an expert on classical music? "She has an implant," I said. "So she can hear really well."

"How do you know?" Kelsey asked.

"People with implants hear better than people with hearing aids. My mother told me."

"Why didn't you get one?" Miranda said.

"They're only for deaf people. The rest of us have hearing aids."

"But if you can hear better with a cochlear implant, shouldn't you have one?" Miranda asked.

Now I remembered why we didn't eat with Miranda and Kelsey last year. Miranda asks too many questions and Kelsey talks nonstop. "I don't know," I said.

"I'm going to go ask Sierra about her implant," Miranda said, stuffing a half-eaten sandwich into her bag. Kelsey fished it out and began finishing it.

"Don't!" I said.

Kelsey gave me a weird look.

"Not you," I said. "Eat whatever you want. I was talking to Miranda." I gave Miranda my best stern look. "Don't ask Sierra questions. Nobody likes to talk about their hearing stuff."

The look didn't work. "You don't like talking about it," Miranda said. "Maybe she's different." Then she walked away, toward Sierra.

"We should go with her," Kelsey said.

"You can," I said. "I've gotten enough dirty looks from Sierra today."

"How about we watch from over there," Lucy said, pointing to a corner of the school. "Come on."

We followed her. Sierra was on a bench, eating daintily from a container with a spoon. She reminded me of a life-sized American Girl doll at a tea party. Miranda had plopped down next to her. From where we were watching, Sierra seemed as if she was actually interested in Miranda.

"Sierra's laughing," Lucy said.

"Maybe she's happy someone is talking to her," Kelsey said.

"I tried to talk to her," I said.

"You stared at her," Lucy said. "You hate when people stare at you."

Why do people who are supposed to be your friends have to make you feel worse than you already do?

"Oh my goodness," Lucy said.

Stephanie and Emma had squeezed onto the bench. They were smiling as if they were best friends with Sierra. Miranda looked as if she wanted to leave, but Sierra put her hand on Miranda's leg to get her to stay. Then Emma tossed her head back and laughed, and so did Stephanie. The next thing I knew all the grade six girls were gathered around the bench fussing over Sierra and her perfect hair and her cochlear implant, and Kelsey, Lucy and I were stuck watching from our hiding spot against the school, alone.

Chapter 5

Most clubs don't start till the second week of school, but Miss Fielding was in a hurry with the running club. She had scheduled a practice for the first day. I practically had to drag Lucy. She could spend a half hour putting her books away. She says it's because she's meticulous, but we both know it's because she's a dawdler. Not wanting to be in running club didn't help.

By the time we got to the gym, Miss Fielding had already started her presentation. She is tiny, like a gymnast. Her hair is as short as a boy's because she shaved it last spring to raise money for cancer research.

The first race was next Wednesday at Laurier Park. Miss Fielding said she didn't expect any of us to win. She just wanted us to do our best, because the point of running club was to be fit and enjoy being outdoors in the fall. I wasn't sure whether or not to believe her. Would she really not care if none of us did well?

Stephanie and Emma cared. They high-fived each other as if to say Miss Fielding was going to be more than pleasantly surprised because not only were they going to win every race, they would also be heading to the Olympics when running club ended. Miss Fielding stopped talking and looked at them.

"We're in the Tornadoes," Stephanie explained.

"The best running club in Edmonton," Emma added.

"That's terrific," Miss Fielding said. "We can always use leaders to set good examples."

Lucy poked me. "This is going to be worse than I thought," she whispered.

It was bad enough Stephanie and Emma acted like they were better than everybody—it appeared it might be true. They were certainly dressed for the part, with their brand-new running shoes and track-suits. As awful as it was to admit, they probably were the fastest girls in the school.

If only Lucy and I could do something better than them, something public and that counted, like rescuing orphans from a fire or solving global warming.

"It's just a few days a week," I whispered back. "And it'll be finished by October."

"I might not last that long."

"Or maybe you'll be really good at it!"

She gave me a you're-crazy look.

Miss Fielding was talking about stretching. "We better pay attention," I whispered as I tried to reach my toes, but they seemed very far away.

"Why?" Lucy replied. "I'll be dead before any of this happens. I can't even run half a block."

"We'll do a short warm-up run today," Miss Fielding announced. "We have some volunteers to help out, so if you have to walk that's fine. A volunteer will make sure you're not alone."

The volunteers were junior high kids. Miranda and Kelsey's sister, Jackie, was one of them.

"I'll run with the back of the group," Miss Fielding said. She turned to a tall, strong-looking junior high girl, Sasha, and asked her to run up front. Then she said, "Stephanie and Emma, you run with Sasha."

Stem took off as if they'd been shot from a cannon. If I didn't hate them so much, I'd have been impressed. Tyler, a bunch of grade five and four kids, and Miranda and Kelsey followed.

Miss Fielding was encouraging to me and Lucy. She patted Lucy on the shoulder and said, "Good job." To me she said, "You have a nice ride."

"A nice ride?" I said.

"Stride," she said, more loudly. "You have a long stride."

Was I supposed to say thank you?

"Jim Ryun wears hearing aids," she said.

Again, I had no idea what she was talking about. "Who?"

"Jim Ryun. First American high school student to run a mile in under four minutes. In 1964."

Was she telling me I could run fast because I had hearing aids?

"He lost his hearing when he was a kid," she went on. "Measles."

"I was born this way," I said. I guess that meant I wouldn't be running a mile in under four minutes.

Miss Fielding looked like she was going to say something more, but Lucy didn't give her a chance.

"I. Have. To. Stop," she said. Her face was so red, I could practically feel the heat radiating off it. "My chest hurts," she panted. "And my legs feel like logs."

"Let's stretch," Miss Fielding said. She bent Lucy over so her arms dangled near her feet like a rag doll's.

"I hate this," she said, crumpling to the ground. "I can't do it. I hate my mother."

"It's okay, Lucy," I said, helping her up. "We don't have to run the whole way, remember?"

"It takes time to build endurance," Miss Fielding said. "In a month you will amaze yourself."

"But the first race is next week," Lucy said.

"Don't put pressure on yourself," Miss Fielding said. "You don't have to do the race."

"I do," Lucy said. It was hard to tell whether her body was heaving because she was fighting back sobs or if she was still out of breath. "My mother said so."

"If you're not ready, I'll talk to your mom," Miss Fielding said. "But let's keep walking so your muscles don't get stiff."

My legs felt twitchy. I wasn't tired or sore. It was as if I hadn't run at all. If Lucy hadn't been there, I would have kept running.

After we had walked a little way on the path, Miss Fielding looked at her watch. "Everyone will be coming back soon. Let's head in."

"Do we have to run?" Lucy asked.

"Not if you don't want to," Miss Fielding said.

A look crossed Lucy's face. I knew we were thinking the same thing: Stem was at the front of the pack. If they saw how slow we were on their way back, they'd never leave us alone.

"I'll try," Lucy said. We had to stop a couple of times, but we reached the school before the rest of the club was even out of the river valley.

Miss Fielding made us do more stretches. "Drink lots of liquids, both of you," she said as we finished up and grabbed our backpacks. "See you at practice tomorrow."

We crossed the street and saw her jog up the block to meet everyone.

"Let's get out of here," Lucy said, speeding up. "I don't care if I get a cramp. I don't want to see Stephanie and Emma again today."

Chapter 6

At school the next morning, Lucy and I found notes in our cubbies with stick-figure drawings of two people wearing tracksuits and saying, "I'm tired" and, "Why is jogging so hard?" I looked up. Stem was pointing at us and giggling.

"I can't wait till we start getting homework so they'll have something useful to do with their time," I said to Lucy.

"Who knew they were such awful artists?" Lucy folded the drawing into an airplane and put it on Stephanie's desk. "You left your artwork in my cubby," she said.

"And you left yours in mine," I said, dropping my note on Emma's desk.

We slipped into our seats as Mrs. Shewchuk came up the aisle. When she saw the airplane, she said, "Stephanie, I expect better from you. We don't throw paper airplanes in grade six." Stephanie tried to explain, but Mrs. Shewchuk balled up the paper, dropped it into the recycling box and told her to stop making excuses and get to work.

I opened my desk and pretended to look for something so no one would see how hard I was laughing. When I had calmed down, I went to give my FM to Mrs. Shewchuk.

"Thank you, Addy," she said, as if I had done her a favor. She reached toward Sierra, who was behind me with her boom mic. "And thank you, Sierra."

I smiled, but Sierra didn't make eye contact. She turned and was in her seat so fast you'd have thought she had pulled a Harry Potter and apparated into it.

Emma sat behind her. She poked Sierra on the shoulder and tried to hand her a note. Sierra looked confused and turned back to her book. Emma poked her again.

If you're hard of hearing and someone is talking to you, you can pretend you can't hear them. But nobody can ignore a poke. And Emma kept poking.

Sierra started squirming. That's when Mrs. Shewchuk noticed.

"Emma, keep your hands to yourself," she said.

If it had been me, I'd have been embarrassed for the rest of the day, but not Emma. By the time novel study ended and current events began, she was back in suck-up mode.

The current events topic was a newspaper story about a Saskatchewan town that had banned competitive teams. Nobody had to try out anymore; everybody got to play, no matter how skilled they were.

"It's supposed to make it fair, but it's not," Emma said. "Because if you're really good, you should get to play with other really good kids. That's how you get better."

I thought about the kids who weren't really good. Didn't they deserve to get better?

"Addy?" Mrs. Shewchuk looked down at me. "You look as if you have something to say."

"I think Emma is right," I said. "The only way you get better is if you're challenged. Everybody should be challanged—so kids who aren't as good should get to play with the ones who are, because they'll learn more that way."

Emma went from looking pleased with herself to looking as if a thunderstorm was brewing under her skin. Her face turned red and her eyes got squinty.

Mrs. Shewchuk called on Tyler.

"I think…um, I think…" He was staring at me. He couldn't remember my name.

"Addy," Mrs. Shewchuk said.

"Yeah. I think Addy is right, everyone should have a chance to play with more skilled kids. But I think Emma had a point—"

He remembered Emma's name and not mine?

He looked at Emma. "If you play with kids who aren't very good, you get worse," he said.

Actually, that wasn't what Emma had said. But either she had a worse memory than Tyler or she didn't want to tell him he was wrong, because she didn't say anything. It was Mrs. Shewchuk who corrected him. Then Tyler said he still thought good kids should play with good kids and bad kids— that's what he said, bad kids—should play with bad kids, which made me decide he wasn't so cute after all.

Mrs. Shewchuk interrupted him before he had a chance to say "bad kids" again. She told him to use the term "less skilled," which now everybody would know was teacher-talk for "bad."

After that, Henry said everyone should have a chance to play because that was more fair, and Kelsey and Miranda agreed with Henry. He beamed as if he'd won the Stanley Cup. Lucy said competing took the fun out of everything, and then the bell rang and it was time for recess.

The first thing I noticed when Lucy and I got to the playground was Emma and Stephanie hanging around Sierra. They were talking with their hands and smiling big— and what was that? Was Stephanie stroking Sierra's hair?

"What is she doing?" Lucy asked.

"Touching her hair."

"That is weird," Lucy said. "I don't even think Stephanie and Emma touch each other's hair."

Then Sierra began stroking her own hair. When she stopped, Stephanie and Emma looked at her hand. What was going on?

"She's showing them her implant," Miranda announced. She had come up behind me just as I realized it wasn't Sierra's hair Stephanie was touching, it was the transmitter. Sierra must have taken it off so they could touch it. I wondered what it felt like. And could Sierra hear? Probably not, because in a second it was back on her head.

"Did you know implants cost as much as a house?" Miranda said.

"What?" Lucy and I asked at the same time.

"I heard Sierra telling Stephanie and Emma how much her implant cost."

"Why?" I asked. Was she trying to impress them? Make them think she was important because she had expensive stuff inside and outside her deaf head? Did she think she was better than everyone because her head was worth as much as a house? Who even knew how much a house cost? Who cared?

"How much do your hearing aids cost?" Miranda asked.

"I don't know," I said. "I don't pay for them. And I'll bet she doesn't know how much her implant costs either. She was asleep when she got it."

"Really?" Miranda looked surprised.

"You have to have an operation to get an implant. They can't cut your head open when you're awake."

"They cut her head open?" Miranda was shocked.

"How else do you think they get it in?"

"That sounds scary," Miranda said. "I think you're better off."

"Me too," I said.

Chapter 7

Our next running club practice on Thursday started out slightly better than the first one. Stephanie and Emma were in such a hurry to be first, they didn't pay attention to Lucy and me.

I thought maybe we could keep up with them. But two blocks after we started, Lucy looked like she was going to have a heart attack. She was huffing like my grandparents' neighbor who has emphysema and is permanently attached to an oxygen tank.

I wanted to say something encouraging, but what can you tell your best friend when she is torturing herself other than, "Stop that! Now!" which I didn't think would be helpful.

Miss Fielding had a better idea. She put her arm around Lucy's shoulder. "Let's walk a little."

Lucy shook her head. Sweat dripped off her face.

"It's good to take a break," Miss Fielding said. "We'll run again when you're ready."

That worked. Lucy bent over, sweaty and panting. I wished we could keep going.

"Why don't you catch up with the rest," Miss Fielding said to me, pointing off in the distance to where the running club was heading into the river valley.

Could she see inside my head too, like Mrs. Shewchuk? I looked at Lucy again. Her hair was matted to her forehead and cheeks. "I'll stay," I said. "Friends stick together."

When I said "friends," Lucy gave me a pained, wheezy smile. "You should go," she said. "It's okay. I'm so slow."

"Uh-uh," I said. "I probably couldn't keep up anyway."

I had never lied to Lucy before. I wondered if she could tell, but she was grimacing again and I was pretty sure it was because her lungs hurt, or whatever it is that hurts when you run more than you want, or can.

Dried leaves covered the path, which was wide enough so we could run side by side. The sun washed through the canopy of trees. A light breeze cooled the air.

"Do you want to keep going?" I asked, hopefully.

Lucy nodded. "I just don't know for how long. My chest still hurts." She took a deep breath and squeezed out two more words. "Let's go."

We headed into the river valley, but the rest of the club was out of sight. I meant to stay with Lucy and Miss Fielding, but it was as if I forgot where I was and who I was with. I glided down the path and couldn't hear anything except my feet on the packed dirt and dead leaves.

The first cross-country meet was next Wednesday, one week away. The farthest I had run without stopping was four hundred meters. Miss Fielding told us the race at Laurier Park would be twelve hundred meters.

I wondered if I should practice on the weekend, but with who? Mom didn't like to exercise. Dad worked all weekend. There was no way I'd ask Lucy.

I wondered if Stephanie and Emma practiced together. They wouldn't call it practice though.

They would call it *training*. Training was important. Everything they did was important. Being friends with Sierra was one more important thing. Because everyone knew cochlear implants were more important than hearing aids.

What I didn't get was why Sierra wanted to be friends with them. If I had been her, the new deaf kid in a school full of hearing kids, and there was a girl with hearing aids, especially a nice, friendly girl, I'd want to talk to her. We would be friends because we had something important in common.

Birds of a feather flock together. That was another of my grandmother's sayings. I guess Sierra had never heard it.

I was starting to get hot and a little tired, but I wanted to run at least to the bridge at the end of the path. Then I could turn back without having to see Stem. It would be bad enough watching them zip past me at Wednesday's race. At least today I could get back to the school before them and pretend I was better, even if it meant sort of cheating by turning back early.

The wind sounded strange. It seemed to be wailing, even though there was only a slight breeze. Then I realized it was a siren. I couldn't tell if it was an ambulance, fire truck or police car. It never occurred to me the wailing could be a person.

Then I saw some teenagers running toward me, and I realized Lucy and Miss Fielding weren't behind me. I turned around and around, but all I saw were the teenagers passing me as if I were invisible. Where was Lucy? Where was Miss Fielding?

I ran as fast as I could back up the path. That's when I saw Lucy, flat on the ground surrounded by Miss Fielding, two strangers and a yapping, out-of-control dog. One of the strangers turned out to be a medical student on her afternoon run. The other was an old bald man whose crazy dog had run into Lucy, knocking her over and twisting her ankle. If I had a dog, I'd keep it on a leash. A short leash.

Lucy was trying not to cry. The bald man was wagging his finger at the dog, yelling, "Bad, bad Custard!" If Lucy hadn't looked so awful, I would have laughed. Custard. What kind of name was that?

The medical student was looking at Lucy's ankle. "It's probably just a sprain, but to be sure you should take her to a clinic," she said to Miss Fielding.

I crouched next to Lucy. "Does it hurt?" I asked. She nodded.

I squeezed her hand. "I'm sorry. I guess I was running too fast," I said.

She looked at Custard, who was jumping around so wildly I was surprised he hadn't pulled the bald man over. "I should probably thank him."

"Don't look *too* happy," I said. "Your mother may think you fell on purpose."

She sniffled loudly and wiped her nose. "Oww," she moaned. "It really hurts."

"That's good," I said. "You fooled me. Can you get up?"

"I'm not kidding," she said. "It really does hurt. Almost as much as running."

Lucy stayed home from school the next day. The medical student was right—she had a slight sprain. Lucy's doctor said she shouldn't stand on it for at least two days. By Sunday it wasn't nearly as swollen, but it still hurt and she needed crutches. Joanne wanted her to buck up, run through the pain. That's what Joanne would have done.

"Did you know the week before I was to run in my first triathlon I tripped over your tricycle in the front hall and sprained my ankle?" she said as she hovered over us. We were in Lucy's family room, watching ABC Kids.

"Yes, you told me on the way home from the clinic, remember?" Lucy said.

Joanne's eyes were all sparkly. "Well, I didn't tell Addy." She looked awfully happy for someone who was about to tell a story about how she was almost crippled on the eve of her debut as a champion triathlete.

"Mom, I've heard it a million times," Lucy said. "I can tell Addy. Later. Right now we're watching TV."

When she left, Lucy rolled her eyes and asked if I'd go to the garage and find the tricycle so she could trip over it and reinjure herself, at least until running club was over.

"Do you want to run in the race?" she asked.

I shrugged.

"I think you should," she said. "I won't be there, so you can go as fast as you want."

"I'm not that fast," I said.

"You're faster than me," she pointed out. And then she laughed and said, "Everybody is faster than me."

Joanne came back carrying a brand-new water bottle with *CamelBak* stamped across the bottom in white letters. It looked expensive.

"I bought this for Lucy, for the race, but since she won't be running, I thought I'd give it to you for luck."

"You should save it. She'll be better by next week." I tried to make Lucy take the bottle, but she pushed it back at me. "Besides, I don't know if I'm going to run. Maybe I'll wait so we can run together."

"Of course you should compete!" Joanne said. "You've been training."

"For two days," I said. "I don't think that counts." I held out the bottle, but Joanne pushed it back at me like Lucy had.

"I'll buy Lucy another one," she said. "It's nice to have something new for a race—as long as it's not new runners. Did I tell you what happened when I tried to wear new runners in my first half marathon?"

"You got a blister so bad you couldn't wear shoes for three weeks," Lucy said.

"Oh, I guess I did tell you," Joanne said.

If I repeated myself as much as she did, I'd be embarrassed.

"Sorry about that," Lucy said when her mother went back to the kitchen. "You don't have to run just because she gave you a water bottle, you know."

"I know."

"But if you do, I'll come and watch."

"Really?"

"Of course," she said. "If it wasn't for me, you wouldn't even be in the running club. It's the least I can do."

Chapter 8

Have you ever seen pictures of factory farms, where all the chickens are squashed together in cages, pinned in by other baby chickens and completely, thoroughly unable to move? That's how I felt at the Laurier Park starting line. Except it wasn't future Kentucky Fried dinners surrounding me, it was grade six girls— hundreds of them pressed together.

Facing us, about twenty meters from the starting line, was a man in a blue Adidas tracksuit. Miss Fielding explained that he was the starter. When he said *ready, set, go*, the twelve-hundred-meter race would begin.

I had never seen so many runners together. What if I got knocked over? Would I be able to get up? Or would the other girls run right over me?

Running in a race without Lucy was a bad idea. I should have waited until she got better. We could have been smushed and crushed together. If you're going to go down, better to go with a friend. That sounds like one of my grandmother's sayings, but I made it up. Just now.

I tipped my head toward the sky and leaned back, as if I was going to do a backbend. If I could look at the sky, maybe I wouldn't feel so—what was the word? *Claus, clausto*—claustrophobic. Fear of small spaces. Just as the word popped into my head, I felt a hand on my back.

"Stand straight and face front, Addy," Miss Fielding said. "The race is about to begin."

Ahead of me, the backs of Stephanie's and Emma's heads were so close I could feel the air shift every time their ponytails swung back and forth. They moved in unison, like windshield wipers in a rainstorm. Like perfect windshield wipers that wouldn't be trampled because, of course, they were in the front row. They could run away from everybody before they got knocked to the ground.

When Miss Fielding had lined us up, she had said, "Fastest in front. There's not enough room for everyone to stand side by side." Then she pushed Stem ahead of everyone else.

All of us wore blue-and-white Mackenzie shirts, but nobody looking at us—Kelsey and Miranda were in the second row next to me—would think we were on the same team. Stephanie and Emma were stretching as if they were warming up for the world championships. Kelsey was hopping up and down to see how many people were behind us, and Miranda was trying to talk to me.

"Addy? Have you ever run in a race before?" she yelled.

Emma turned to see what the fuss was about. "Addy's never run more than one hundred meters at one time," she said. I could tell she was thinking there was no way I would make it to twelve hundred.

"It's okay if you walk, you know," Stephanie said, as if she were talking to a kindergartner who had gotten lost on the way to the bathroom. "Lots of girls can't run that far. You'll have plenty of company." She looked at Kelsey and Miranda.

I tried to think of something clever to say, but before I had a chance, a loud voice said, "Okay, girls!" It must have been the man in the Adidas tracksuit, but I couldn't see him any longer because more girls had filled the front row and were completely blocking my view.

I couldn't hear him very well either. A collective yell rose up around me. A lot of girls jammed their fingers in their ears. I guess the yelling bothered them too. And then there was a horrible loud cracking noise like a car engine backfiring, and the row of girls ahead of me swept forward.

I had forgotten about the starting gun. Why hadn't Miss Fielding reminded me? Lucy was lucky she was on the sidelines. I wished I was, but the girls behind me were pushing me forward.

That's when I started to run as fast as I could. If I didn't, I'd be like those people who get flattened at soccer games in England or Brazil, or wherever soccer is called football, and there are stampedes at the stadiums.

How long would it take to run twelve hundred meters? Jim Ryun could probably do it in three minutes. But me? Would it take ten minutes? A half hour? I should have run around the block yesterday and timed myself so I'd know.

My legs felt heavy. Now I understood why Lucy hated running. But I couldn't quit. I had to get to the finish line, and running would get me there faster.

Where were Stephanie and Emma? Probably at the finish. I pulled a corner of my shirt up to mop my face, and when I was done, I realized I was alone. Where was everyone else? Was I lost? Was I last? I was going to be the last one over the finish line, the biggest loser, the one everyone claps extra loud for because they feel bad for her.

I thought about hiding in the bushes until the grade five girls' race started. I could get lost in the middle of them and blend in. But I'd have to sit through the grade six boys' race first. I could imagine my mother at the finish if I didn't show up. She would probably have the RCMP, police helicopters and sniffer dogs out after me. She'd be wailing, "Her batteries must have died and she can't hear me!"

If I was going to be last, at least I could try closing the gap between me and the rest of the losers. But as soon as I sped up, a cramp started spreading across my stomach. What had Miss Fielding said about cramps? *Rub your belly* or *Breathe from your belly*? *Breathe through your mouth* or *Count your breath*?

I was so busy trying to figure out what would make the cramp disappear I was surprised to see people, parents and kids, lining the path, cheering, clapping and shouting.

Had I finished? Already? Mom and Lucy were at the finish line, beaming as if I'd won a gold medal. "You're the first Mackenzie girl across the line!" my mother said. "Good on you, Addy!"

"You beat Stephanie and Emma! You beat them!" Lucy was so excited, she started pounding me on the back.

She was crazy. There was no way I had beat Stem. I was the last to finish.

I was funneled into a chute with rope fences on either side. I stood on my toes to look for Stephanie, Emma, Miranda and Kelsey in the crowd ahead. I couldn't see any of them. They had probably finished so long ago they had gone home.

"Here." Lucy pushed my new water bottle into my hands. "Drink."

In front of me, girls emptied their water bottles over their heads. I opened mine and sipped. The water felt so good sliding down my throat. I wished I could have poured some over my head, but that would wreck my hearing aids.

My mother leaned over the rope and hugged me. "You finished sixteenth, Addy! Out of almost two hundred girls! That's great! You worked so hard!"

"Mom, I'm last," I said. "There is nobody behind me."

"There are more than one hundred and fifty girls behind you," my mother said. She pointed over my shoulder. Girls were pouring across the finish line. A line of sweaty grade sixers, all dumping water over their heads, formed behind me.

"How did that happen?"

"How did what happen?" Lucy asked.

"How did all those people get behind me? I was the slowest person out there."

"She must be hallucinating," Lucy said to my mother, as if I wasn't there. "That happens sometimes when you're tired and sweaty."

"I'm not hallucinating!" I said, and that's when I saw Stem stumble across the finish line and into the chute. They looked more tired than I felt. So much for training with "Edmonton's top running club." There were so many girls between us, I couldn't count them all. Had I really finished ahead of them? And that far ahead?

"You creamed them!" Lucy gasped.

Miss Fielding was waiting for me at the end of the chute. As I collected my ribbon she said, "Very fine job, Adeline Markley. You were a star today."

"Do you want to stay and congratulate the rest of the girls from your team?" Mom asked.

"Oh please, let's," Lucy said.

"I'd rather go home and shower and change my clothes," I said.

"But you finished sixteenth!" Lucy said. "Sixteenth! That's like, like, like—"

"That's like after fifteenth and before seventeenth," I said. "Let's go home."

"But you beat Stephanie and Emma!" Lucy reminded me.

"I think it was a fluke," I said.

"You finished almost fifty people ahead of them," she said. "That's no fluke. You really are fast, Addy."

"I am not," I said.

"You *are*." She looked at her bandaged ankle. "I probably won't be able to run next week."

"But you said it was getting better. I don't want to run alone again."

"You'd be running alone anyway," she said. "Even Stephanie and Emma can't keep up with you."

My mother hugged me. "I think you should stay and celebrate with your team."

"It's okay, really," I said, looking over my shoulder. Stem was coming toward us, arm in arm, smug and sweaty.

First they saw me. Then they saw my ribbon. Suddenly they looked like birthday balloons that had lost their air—not the fun way, whooshing around like missiles, but the slow, depressing way, like balloons three months after the party.

"You finished?" Stephanie asked.

"How did you get ahead of us?" Emma demanded.

"Hello, Stephanie and Emma," my mother said.

"Hi, Mrs. Markley," they said in one voice, looking quickly back at me for an explanation.

Lucy looked as if she was going to burst. "She got ahead of you because she finished before you," she announced, looping her arm through mine.

I held up my ribbon. I wasn't feeling enthusiastic. I was embarrassed.

"Where'd you finish?" Stephanie asked in an I-don't-believe-you voice.

I pointed. "Over there, at the finish line, same as you." Tons more girls had lined up. They spilled out the back of the chute.

If an adult wasn't there, Emma probably would have said something awful. Instead she and Stephanie looked at each other and then at me. But not at my face. At my hearing aids.

"I heard you fine," I said, even though it was getting loud. As more girls finished, their parents, grandparents, brothers, sisters, coaches and teammates crowded toward the finish line. Everyone was talking and laughing at the same time, creating a steady hum and buzz. It was distracting.

"What *place* did you finish?" Emma said.

"Sixteenth," Lucy said.

"We were asking Addy," Stephanie said.

"Sixteenth," I said.

Emma huffed. "Well, we all got the same color ribbon," she said and stomped off with Stephanie.

Lucy laughed. It's less a laugh, really, than a weird sound she makes when she's nervous or excited—a cross between a donkey, a rooster and a person with bad lungs gulping for air. You can't hear it and not stop to see where it's coming from. Everyone nearby turned, even Stephanie and Emma. Lucy waved at them. She tried to grab my arm and make me wave too, but I wasn't in the mood.

"What's wrong?" she asked.

"I'm not that good of a runner!" My face felt hotter than it had when I crossed the finish line. "I didn't even run the whole time!"

That got more attention than Lucy's laugh.

"What did you just say?" Emma asked, pulling Stephanie along as she stomped back toward us.

"I said, I didn't run the whole way. I got tired. So I walked in the middle."

"You cheated!" Emma snapped.

Now everyone near us was staring.

"I did not cheat!" I said. "I followed the same course Miss Fielding took us on during our warm-up!" At least, I thought I did.

"You don't have to yell, Addy," Stephanie said. "*We're* not hard of hearing."

My mother's eyes grew hard, and her voice was cold. "Stephanie, that was uncalled for."

Stephanie's face turned more shades of red than I knew existed. "I'm sorry," she mumbled.

"I did not cheat!" I repeated. "I am not a cheater."

My mother started to say something, but Miss Fielding appeared.

"What's this about cheating?" she asked.

"Addy walked," Stephanie and Emma said.

"You told me I could," I reminded Stephanie. "In the starting line. You said, 'You don't have to run the whole way. Lots of kids can't run that far. You'll have company.'"

I tried to say it in the voice she'd used—the snotty, I'm-better-than-you tone—in case Miss Fielding thought she had said it to be helpful.

"Walking isn't cheating," Miss Fielding said.

"But she beat us," Stephanie said.

"Yeah," Emma said. "How could she beat us if she walked?"

"She didn't walk the whole race." Miss Fielding looked at me. "Did you, Addy?"

"No. I just walked until I wasn't as tired. Then I ran."

"So there's your answer, girls," Miss Fielding said. "Addy's fast."

"Faster than you," Lucy said, but not as quietly as she should have.

Miss Fielding gave her a that-wasn't-appropriate look.

I was so confused. Miss Fielding was defending me? I wasn't even sure *I* should be defending me. How did Miss Fielding know if I was fast? I hadn't even finished one training run with running club yet. I wanted to say, *Stephanie and Emma may be right. I might have cheated. By accident.*

I tried to remember when and where I could have gone off the path. I was sure I had followed the orange cones marking the course. But I hadn't seen people the whole time. Maybe I accidentally took a shortcut. I'm not always good at following directions.

"Do I have to give back my ribbon?" I asked Miss Fielding.

"Why would you have to do that?" she asked.

I shrugged.

Miss Fielding put her arm around my shoulder. "Just because you walked doesn't mean you couldn't make up the time running, Addy. You've obviously got speed. We just need to work on your training so you'll have the endurance to match. You can do it. You're off to a fine start."

Chapter 9

I tried not to look at Stephanie and Emma the next day, but the problem with a small school is it's hard to avoid anyone. Especially when they go out of their way to be annoying. The more I tried not to look at them, the more annoying they were. Before the first recess bell, they were whispering and pointing at me. I know they were telling Tyler I had cheated, because he glared at me.

Then, when we were at our cubbies, Stem started throwing wads of paper at me. On each piece they had written a big letter *C*. If Mrs. Shewchuk had been there, they never would have dared, but Mrs. Shewchuk had horrible timing and picked the day after the Laurier race to get sick.

The substitute, Mr. Angelo, did not look like a teacher. With hair to his shoulders, a Hawaiian shirt and a gold chain around his neck, he looked as if he belonged at a tropical resort. When he put on Sierra's boom mic, he reminded me of a rap singer.

Mr. Angelo didn't know how to be a teacher either. In current events, he let everybody say whatever they wanted. Henry had brought in an article about a family from Indonesia that was being deported. The family had hired a lawyer to get them refugee status when they arrived fourteen years earlier, but the Immigration people said the lawyer hadn't filed papers and the family was in Canada illegally.

"That sucks," Tyler said. "It wasn't their fault."

"I think they lied," Henry said. "They wanted to stay in Canada without applying to."

The family had three kids, all born in Canada. The oldest child was our age.

I raised my hand. "If they hired a lawyer and the lawyer didn't do his job, shouldn't the lawyer get into trouble?"

Stephanie interrupted before I could ask my next question. "How do we even know they hired a lawyer?" she said. "Sometimes people say one thing when everyone knows they cheated."

My face started burning. I raised my hand again. So did Kelsey and Miranda, but I started talking before Mr. Angelo called on anyone because, really, it was still my turn.

"The article said they hired a lawyer," I said. "But now nobody can find him. Maybe he wasn't a real lawyer, but they didn't know any better because they had just arrived here."

"They didn't follow the rules," Stephanie said. "You can't blame someone else because you cheated."

I wasn't blaming anyone. And I didn't cheat. If Mrs. Shewchuk had been here, she would have told Stephanie to stick to the subject. Not Mr. Angelo.

"That's a good point," he said. "If you don't know you're cheating, does it count as cheating?"

He called on Kelsey, whose hand was still raised. "If the kids are Canadian, shouldn't they get to stay?" she said. "It's not fair to make them go some place they've never been. They probably don't even speak whatever language is spoken there."

Mr. Angelo didn't answer. Instead, he called on Sierra. "My cousin in New York had a nanny from Haiti," she said. "She had to go back because Immigration said she was an illegal alien. After that my cousin didn't have a nanny."

"You have a cousin in New York?" Tyler interrupted.

"Tyler, we're talking about immigration," Mr. Angelo said.

"I'd like to immigrate to New York," Tyler said, and everyone laughed, even Mr. Angelo.

I raised my hand again. "Was there an article in the New York paper when the nanny got deported?" I asked.

Sierra and Mr. Angelo looked confused. "Maybe people get deported all the time," I said. "So how come this story"—I pointed to the photocopy on my desk—"was in the paper?"

"That's a good question," Mr. Angelo said. "Why does anything get into the newspaper? What makes something newsworthy? That's a good current events topic."

And just like that he changed the subject. I could have done a better job leading the discussion.

But apparently the rest of the class had short attention spans too.

Sierra raised her hand again. "I don't think there was an article about Memmy," she said, looking at me. "You're right—probably people get deported all the time. But maybe not whole families. If something is unusual, it's newsworthy."

She tucked her hair behind her ear so everyone could see her implant. "When I got my implant, I lived in Nanaimo. I was the first kid there to have one, so the newspaper wrote an article about me."

Nobody had ever written an article about me. I wondered if Sierra had made up the thing about the deported nanny to work something into the discussion about her implant.

"What was it like to get that kind of attention, Sierra?" Mr. Angelo asked.

"It was neat, but a little embarrassing." Her voice got quiet. "Whenever I was out after that, people stared at me. I wasn't sure if it was because they'd seen my picture, or because they'd never seen an implant. My mom said if people stared, it was because they were curious, so I should tell them about it. Sometimes I go to conferences and talk about my implant."

Sometimes I go to conferences and talk about my implant. I looked at Lucy so we could make she-is-so-full-of-herself faces, but Lucy was paying attention. To Sierra.

"I was on the news in Victoria when I was seven because I won a chess tournament," Henry said. "It was newsworthy because before I won, only teenagers and old people had won."

"When I was in grade two, I won the district spelling bee and got my picture in the paper," Tyler said.

And that's how the rest of current events went, from talking about immigration and deportation to everyone taking turns bragging about when they had been on TV or in the newspaper or invited to speak at conferences.

I had never done any of that. I spent the discussion doodling in the margins of my scribbler.

At the end of the day when Sierra and I picked up our FMS, Mr. Angelo gushed over Sierra's boom mic. "I wanted to be a disc jockey when I was a kid," he said to her. "I kind of felt like one today. What a cool thing."

"It's really expensive," she said. "It's probably more expensive than what a DJ uses. It's the best technology there is."

I reached for my transmitter. It looked almost exactly like Sierra's, the same shape as a fish stick and about as big, but Mr. Angelo didn't notice. He was too busy being impressed with Sierra's boom mic, even though the only reason she had an extra mic was because the one in the transmitter wasn't powerful enough for her rotten hearing. What was so impressive about that?

Chapter 10

"I think he is the worst substitute we've ever had," I announced to Lucy on the way home.

"Uh-uh," she said. "Don't you remember the one in grade three who yelled and jumped on her desk when she saw a wasp on the window? And it was on the *outside*."

"Oh, yeah! Mrs. Finchley!" I remembered because her name sounded like a bird, and she had practically flown onto her desk. "But she wasn't bad, just weird."

That's when Stephanie and Emma appeared on either side of us, like police officers surrounding their suspects. "Hanging around with the cheater?" Emma said.

"She's not a cheater," Lucy said. "She's faster than you."

"What are they even doing here?" I asked. "Don't they have to train with the best running club in Edmonton?"

"We can hear you, Addy," Stephanie said. "We're not deaf."

"Neither am I," I said. "And I'm not a cheater. I could beat you anytime."

As soon as the words were out of my mouth, I wondered where they had come from and why I had said them.

Emma thought I was challenging her. "Let's go," she said. "Now!" She took off, her backpack bumping on her back, her ponytail swinging. Stephanie was at her heels.

Lucy and I watched, shaking our heads. When they turned around—probably to see how far ahead of me they were and gloat—I waved. That's when they came back toward us, angry and yelling.

"What are they squawking about?" I asked Lucy.

"Stephanie called you a chicken, and Emma said you couldn't beat them if their legs were tied together."

"There's an idea," I said. "Maybe we ought to tie their legs together. And stuff socks in their mouths so they can't talk."

"Too scared to race?" Stephanie called out as she got closer. She was so loud that some moms and kids on the other side of the street turned to see what was going on.

"Give me your backpack," Lucy said.

"Huh?"

"Give me your backpack. When they get back here, say, 'ready, set, go,' and take off and show them how fast you are. You'll beat them because you'll have the head start."

"I don't need a head start," I said. "I'm not going to race them."

"Why not? Just show them you're faster and they'll leave us alone."

"I don't feel like it," I said. "Besides, my backpack is too heavy for you. You're still on crutches."

"Come on, Addy."

"No," I said.

Stephanie and Emma were just a few steps away. They had heard everything.

"Afraid to lose?" Emma said, her nose suddenly so close to mine I could bite it.

I pushed past her, and she stumbled.

"Hey, watch what you're doing!" Stephanie said.

I switched off my hearing aids before I could hear another word. I walked as quickly as I could. I didn't care that Lucy couldn't keep up.

When I felt something pushing into my back, I turned and flipped on my hearing aids. Lucy pulled the end of her crutch away and stuck it back onto the sidewalk. Stephanie and Emma had crossed the street. Finally. We were rid of them.

"You walk pretty fast for someone with a sprained ankle," I said.

She poked at her ankle with a crutch. "It's not really sprained anymore. But don't tell."

"When did it stop hurting?"

"A couple of days ago."

"You could have done the run!"

"Not really," she said. "I mean, it's not that good. And I'm still really slow."

"So? It would have been better if you'd run with me. It was scary alone."

"You weren't alone! There were almost two hundred people in that race!"

"But none of them was my friend."

"I wouldn't have been able to keep up," she said.

"I could have gone slowly. I'd rather run with you than alone."

Lucy's eyes widened. "I just thought of something! A way for you not to have to run alone!"

"Yeah," I said. "You run with me. *I* just thought of that, remember?"

"No, something better!" I hadn't seen her this excited since we got free popsicles on Whyte Avenue in August. "Your FM. I can hold it and talk to you while you're running. I can keep you company and not have to torture myself!"

I shook my head. "Yeah. You'll be torturing me instead. You know I hate having a voice in my head."

Lucy looked hurt.

"Anyone's voice. Not just yours."

"But I'm your friend!"

"I like hearing your voice through the air. Only crazy people hear voices in their heads. I'm not crazy. But I will be if I use the FM all the time."

"Okay," she said glumly. "I just thought it was a good idea."

"A good idea is for you to run with me. Or walk. You just said your ankle doesn't hurt anymore. If you don't come to running club tomorrow, I'm telling your mother."

"You wouldn't."

"I would."

Chapter 11

The next race was at Hawrelak Park, the biggest park in Edmonton. I hadn't seen Lucy so scared since her mother took us to see *Avatar* during Christmas break in grade four. Joanne kept leaning over her popcorn and saying, "What are you so afraid of? It's about nature!" And I was thinking, What's so natural about people with blue faces and tails?

"Were there this many girls at the last race?" Lucy asked as she hopped from one foot to another in the starting line.

"I don't think so," I said. "But don't be nervous."

"I'm not," she said. "I'm stretching. My mother told me to. I think this is what she said to do." She crouched like a cougar about to attack. "Or maybe not." She went back to hopping. "You said we don't have to run the whole way, right?"

She didn't think she was nervous, but she sure was acting like it. Or maybe I was the nervous one.

"I think you've stretched enough." I put my hand on her shoulder to hold her still. "You probably shouldn't use up all your energy."

"We can walk, right?"

"Yes!" I said for the gazillionth time.

She looked hurt. "You don't have to yell."

"I'm sorry," I said.

I didn't think I'd be nervous. It was my second race. I knew what to expect. But I couldn't help it. There were four rows of girls between us and the front line of starters. Even this far back, Stephanie and Emma stuck out like fake trees at a Christmas-tree farm. I wondered, if Lucy's ankle was still hurt and she couldn't run, would I have wanted to be up front with them?

"I'm glad you're back here with me," Lucy said. She hugged me. "I'm lucky to have a friend like you."

"Grade six girls!" It must have been the man in the Adidas tracksuit, but I couldn't see him because of all the girls in front of me.

"Who said that?" Lucy demanded.

"The starter guy."

"The starter guy?"

"The ready-set-go guy," I said. "The one with the gun."

"The gun?"

"The starting gun! You were at the race last week—remember, at the very beginning, there was a gun?"

Lucy shook her head.

"Weren't you listening?"

"I wasn't running," she said. "I didn't have to listen."

"Well, there was a starting gun then and there's one now, and he's about to pull the trigger." Before I had a chance to turn off my hearing aids there was a *bang!* and everyone took off. It didn't bother me nearly as much this time, but I wasn't sure whether it was because I was expecting it or because I was too busy with Lucy. Everyone else took off. Not her. I had to pull on her arm or she would have been there when the boys lined up ten minutes later for their race. But once she was running, she was so quick she surprised herself *and* me.

"You're doing great!" I said as we passed a bunch of girls from the row in front of us.

Maybe we could catch up to Stem and wave as we passed them. That would be fun—and it would make them mad. But we wouldn't care, because we would be catching up to the faster girls and passing them too. We would get real ribbons, fourth or fifth place. Not first—we wouldn't be that fast.

We were doing so much better than I had expected. Lucy was running hard and not running out of breath. Somewhere inside of her was an athlete just like her mother. But then she stumbled and stopped, and we had to walk and run the rest of the way. Mostly, though, we walked.

By the time we crossed the finish line, Lucy's face was so hot I could have fried an egg on her chin and made toast on her forehead. I was barely sweating. Which made it doubly horrible when Stem came swaggering over and announced they had finished thirty-fifth and thirty-sixth.

"Guess you didn't take any shortcuts this week, did you?" Stephanie said.

Emma snorted. "No, they took the long-cut."

Kelsey and Miranda finished ninety-seventh and ninety-eighth. Emma and Stephanie stopped high-fiving each other long enough to congratulate them.

Kelsey and Miranda weren't used to Stem being friendly. They looked confused. Or maybe it was because Emma was still snorting.

"You sound like a pig," I muttered.

Emma looked at us. "What?"

"I said, you sound like a pig when you laugh."

"Well, at least I don't run like one," she snapped.

"Actually, you do," I said. Then I grabbed Lucy's hand and pulled her over to where our mothers were waiting.

A farm pig can run almost eighteen kilometers an hour. Wild pigs are faster. Cheetahs are the fastest animals on four feet. Ostriches are the fastest on two. Some cheetahs can run more than two hundred kilometers an hour. Lucy and I were about as fast as two jellyfish in a bowl of pudding.

"I'm sorry I slowed you down," Lucy said. "But I'm glad you ran with me. I never would have finished if it wasn't for you."

"Congratulations, girls!" my mother said. "How'd you do?"

"Lucy finished two hundred twenty-fourth and I finished two hundred twenty-fifth," I said. "That's last." In case she hadn't noticed.

My mother smiled. "I'm proud of you both!" she said. She had the same smile on her face as she did when I finished sixteenth at the first race. That's how good an actress she is.

Joanne would not be a good actress, so it's a good thing she's a bank manager. Instead of congratulating us, she said, "Did you girls have a good time?" which was like asking someone who had broken their leg skiing if they'd had fun on the chairlift. It didn't help when she added, "You'll do even better next week!"

"We couldn't do worse," Lucy said, which is what I was thinking but didn't want to say, because I didn't want to hurt anyone's feelings. I wanted to do better next week, but unless Lucy sprained her ankle again, that probably wouldn't happen.

"Lucy! What kind of attitude is that?" Joanne said. "You get out there and train harder, and you'll knock their socks off next time."

Suddenly Joanne's face changed from uncomfortable to happy. I turned to see what she was looking at. There, behind me, were Stephanie and Emma and their mothers.

"Hello, Sandy!" Joanne said to Stephanie's mom. I couldn't understand how Lucy's mother could be friends with Stephanie's mom when Stephanie was so awful.

When Joanne asked, "How did you girls do?" I wanted to turn off my hearing aids before Stem could answer, but my mother was looking at me. So I had to listen when they said how easy the race was. Then Joanne made excuses about Lucy's ankle and gushed that I was such a good friend to let her finish ahead of me.

Of course my mother agreed. She said I was a sensitive girl due to my hearing aids, and the reason I wore hearing aids was because she had a recessive gene. So, it was all because of her that I was sensitive.

Then Sandy reminded everyone that Stephanie and Emma were in the best running club in Edmonton. Before Stephanie and Emma left, Emma said, "Bye, bye," in a little singsong voice. And then she leaned close to me and whispered, "Cheater. Loser."

Chapter 12

I crossed my fingers, hoping Mrs. Shewchuk would be back the next day, and she was. She hadn't been sick. She'd been at a workshop. When novel study ended, she made us play a game she'd learned.

"This will get you thinking about how stars fit into the solar system," she said. "I'm going to hand each of you a card with a picture of a constellation on one side. On the other side is a picture of half the constellation. You have to find the person whose constellation makes yours whole. Compare pictures, and when you find your partner, stand together and wait for the next instruction."

I got Pisces, the fish. Lucy got Ursa Major, the Great Bear. So did Sarah, who is supposed to be a piano prodigy, but I don't think she is because she never plays in the school talent show.

Henry and Stephanie wound up together, which I thought was pretty funny until it turned out my partner was Sierra. We were the last two to find each other. With everyone talking, the room was so loud I had stopped trying to ask people about their constellation. I guess she had too.

Mrs. Shewchuk explained we were going to use "repurposed items" from the Reuse Centre to make mobiles inspired by our constellations. She showed us some finished samples. My favorite had wires shaped like question marks and strung with beads, and more wire shaped like lions, covered with orange and yellow yarn, for Leo the Lion. I wanted to start right away, but Mrs. Shewchuk said we had to do research first to learn about our constellations.

"We'll be spending the next period in the library at the computer stations. Except Addy and Sierra. Come here, please, girls," Mrs. Shewchuk said.

When we got to her desk, she explained that she wanted us to work on her computer. "With everyone in groups, the library will be noisy," she said. "It will be better in here—quieter."

She pulled another chair up to her desk and motioned for me and Sierra to sit. "I'll get you started, and then I'll go to the library," she said.

"It's okay," Sierra said in what I was starting to think of as her I'm-more-important-than-you voice. "I got a computer like this for Christmas last year, so I know how to use it."

By recess, Lucy was an expert on the Big Dipper and I was an expert on Sierra.

"Did you know slaves used to call the Big Dipper the drinking gourd?" Lucy said as we walked across the playground. "When they escaped, they'd say they were following the drinking gourd because they went north and the North Star is part of the Big Dipper. And the Big Dipper is part of Ursa Major."

"Did you know Sierra is really bossy?" I said. "She wouldn't let me use the computer until Mrs. Shewchuk overheard her saying someone had to be in charge and it should be her. Mrs. Shewchuk had to tell her, 'Sierra, you and Addy are partners. You have to work together.' So I got to be in charge of the keyboard, but she was in charge of me. Every website I went to, she kept saying, 'No, go to this one.' I went to Cool Cosmos without her permission, and she made me go to some Star Trek thing. When it turned out to be as useless as I knew it would be, she said, 'Go back to Cool Cosmos.' She didn't even say please."

"Well, did you find out anything interesting?"

"I found out Sierra can't read lips."

"Anything you can use for your mobile?"

"Sierra won an art prize at her last school. And she moved here because her father got a job at Epcor. She's going to Vancouver next month to give a talk at a cochlear implant conference."

"How are you going to use that for your mobile?" Lucy asked.

"I'm not. She thinks because she won an art prize, she should do everything. I want to use empty tuna cans. If we take the paper off, they'll be kind of silvery and shiny, like stars. Or maybe we can use fish skeletons."

"That's gross. But the tuna can idea is good. Did you tell Sierra?"

I nodded. "She said no way, tuna cans stink. As if I wasn't going to wash them first. I bet we're going to do whatever she wants."

"Remind her that Mrs. Shewchuk said it's a partnership."

"How can you be partners with someone who thinks they know everything?"

"Remind them they don't," Lucy said. "Show her your ideas. Except not the fish skeleton one."

"What are you going to do?

"Something with the drinking gourd song, I think. Sarah can play it on the piano."

"We're supposed to be making mobiles, not putting on concerts," I said.

"She's not going to play it for everybody. Maybe we'll cut sheet music in star shapes. I don't know. We don't have to have a plan yet."

"Go tell that to Sierra." I pointed to the stairs behind the school, where Sierra sat with a sketchpad. "She's making one now. When I told her we didn't have to do it during recess, she said, 'Don't worry. I'll come up with ideas.' Which means we're using hers."

"Then you come up with some too," Lucy said. "I'll help."

Chapter 13

The next day started badly. When I woke up, I put my hearing aids in and they were all staticky. I turned them off and on, but they didn't get better, and then the left one stopped working.

My hearing aids never break, although the summer after I got them, I was swimming in Susie Patrick's pool and her dog ate one and chewed half of the other. I had to borrow a pair from the audiology clinic while I waited for my new ones.

I still have the half-chewed one. Mom keeps it in the hearing-aid box in the kitchen, with batteries and the battery tester and the hearing-aid dryer, which we never use because Alberta is so dry you can feel your skin shriveling when you get out of the bathtub. At least that's what my grandmother says all the time.

I went downstairs and got a new battery. When I took the old one out of my left hearing aid there was brown·slimy stuff on it. There was brown slimy stuff in the battery cage too. I pulled the battery out of the right hearing aid. It was just as bad.

"Mom!" I yelled. She was checking her email. She doesn't like being interrupted, but I knew she'd come if it had to do with my hearing aids.

"Look!" I held out the batteries and hearing aids when she came into the kitchen. "What's that gross brown stuff?"

"It's corrosion," she said, wiping a battery with her finger. "It must be from running—from your sweat. I'll clean it with a Q-tip."

Corrosion? I thought that only happened to cars. My dad called his old car the Corroda. Rust had eaten away so much of the side panels, if you touched them, parts of the car crumbled off. Could that happen to my hearing aids?

"Aren't you going to call the audiologist?" I asked as my mother swabbed the inside of my left hearing aid.

"I'm cleaning your hearing aids, Addy," she said. "I can only do one thing at a time. And the audiologist doesn't open for another twenty minutes. It's only ten after seven."

"Sorry," I said. That's when I noticed the Q-tip, covered with brown stuff. "Gross. I need new batteries."

"Test the old ones first," she said. "They might still work."

According to the battery tester, the batteries were fine. But my hearing aids still crackled. After a couple of minutes, they died again.

"What am I going to do? I can't go to school without them. And we're supposed to be doing a science project. If I'm not there, Sierra will do it herself."

"Is that a bad thing?" Mom was trying to be funny. "Sometimes it's nice to have someone else do the work."

"Yes, it's a bad thing!"

"Calm down, Addy," my mother said gently. It was hard for me to hear her, and she was right next to me. How was I going to hear anything at school? It wasn't as if Mrs. Shewchuk would stand beside my desk all day.

"I am calm! But I'm mad. We're supposed to be making mobiles, and Sierra thinks she's the only one with ideas. She'll probably do the whole thing even if I am there, but if I'm not, it'll be worse."

"Who is Sierra?"

"She's new. She has a cochlear implant."

"You haven't told me about her," my mother said.

"Because she's not my friend."

"Did you know that when you were diagnosed, people used to ask if you were going to get a cochlear implant?"

"I know," I said, in a voice that made my mother give me a warning look. "You've told me. I'm glad I don't have one. If I did, I might be like Sierra and act like I'm better than everyone."

"How exactly does she act?"

"As if she knows everything. Next month she's going to Vancouver to give a talk about cochlear implants."

"Do you want to go to Vancouver to talk about hearing aids?" My mother was serious. If she thought I wanted to talk to a bunch of strangers about my hearing aids, she would find a way to make it happen. She'd even coach me. She would say, "It's like acting."

"No!"

"Addy, please don't use that voice with me."

"It's the only voice I have."

My mother shook her head. "If you don't want to talk to people about your hearing loss, why does it bother you if Sierra does?"

"I just told you, because she thinks she's better than everybody."

"Or maybe she thinks she has something to offer by sharing her experiences," my mother said. "And so do you."

"I don't *want* to talk about my hearing aids at a conference!" I was using that voice again. "I'm sorry. I'm sorry I yelled." I looked at the clock. "It's seven thirty. Can you call the audiologist now? Please?"

By the time I got to school, late, after leaving my broken hearing aids at the audiology clinic, everyone was working on reading responses. Lucy looked up and smiled. Sierra stared and went back to her paper. I wondered if she noticed I was wearing different hearing aids. The loaner pair from the audiologist was blue.

But during science, she didn't say anything, even when I pushed my hair behind my ears the way she did when she wanted people to look at her implant. She was so busy with her sketchpad she barely paid attention when I told her I had an idea for the mobile. She just pointed to her pad and said, "We'll use aluminum pie plates, toilet paper rolls and empty spools from thread, and the frame can be made of—"

"I have an idea," I said more loudly.

"Mine is better," she said. "Look, I've already drawn it. You don't have to do anything."

She sounded like my mother, except my mother had been trying to be funny. "We're supposed to be partners. Like Mrs. Shewchuk said? We're supposed to collaborate."

Sierra sighed loudly. "Okay, what's your idea?"

I had given up on tuna cans. I would never tell Sierra, but she was right, they were smelly. Also hard to cut. I had a new idea. "Hearing-aid batteries. They're shiny. They look like little dots, the way stars do when you look up at them."

"I know what hearing-aid batteries look like," she said in a voice that made it obvious she thought I was stupid. "I use them."

She did? What size? In what part of her implant? And did hers die faster when it was cold, the way mine did? But I didn't ask. She wasn't my friend. I didn't care about her batteries, except for how we could use them for our project.

"I have a bag of dead ones at home," I said. "I'll bring them. You can bring yours."

"Mine are really big," she said, as if that made hers better.

"Fine," I said. "Mine are small. Variety is good. It will make the mobile more interesting."

Chapter 14

The Rundle Park race was that afternoon. My mother was busy, so Lucy's mother drove us. Unlike my mother, Joanne didn't listen to the radio in the car. She gave advice.

"My first coach always said the best thing to do before a race is get angry," she said cheerfully. "The angrier you are, the more adrenaline your body makes, and the more adrenaline your body makes, the faster you go."

In that case, Stephanie and Emma were going to be extra fast. They had been acting weird at school, and by the time we got to the walk-through with Miss Fielding, they were fighting. I couldn't tell why, but it was funny watching them snap at each other.

They looked even madder at the starting line, when they had to stand in the fourth row with the rest of us because the first three rows were so crowded.

"They have so much angry adrenaline they might win," I warned Lucy. "So you know what we have to do?"

"Hold onto their ponytails when the gun goes off?"

"Not give up!"

And Lucy didn't—at least not at first. I talked the whole time, to distract her. After a while I realized I'd been so busy talking and making sure she was okay that I had forgotten about Stem. I knew they were ahead, but how far?

"Have you seen them?" I asked Lucy as we approached another hill. "You don't have to talk. Just nod or shake your head."

Instead, she stopped. "I think I saw them up ahead, but I'm not sure."

"Come on, Lucy." I reached for her hand, but she didn't budge.

"I need to rest. You go. Hurry—everyone's passing you."

The girls who had been behind us ran by. I was glad Stem couldn't see.

"I don't want you to run alone," I said. "Come on, you can do it."

"I can't." Was she going to cry? "I'll start again soon, but you keep going. I know you can."

What if I left her and she didn't finish? She could end up still on the course when the boys' race started. Stem would be awful to her, and then she'd hate running even more. I had to stay.

"We don't have to both come in last," she said. "You're better than I am. You're better than they are. Go! Now. Or I won't be your friend anymore."

I didn't believe her. The girls passing us looked over their shoulders at us.

Lucy pushed me. "I'll see you at the finish. Just go."

So I went. When I looked back, just before I got to the top of the hill, Lucy was still walking. She did something with her arms. It wasn't quite a wave—she was telling me to keep going. I caught up to the girls who had seen her yell at me. I could tell they were staring at me as I passed, but I forced myself to look straight ahead.

I wished I knew how much longer the race was. I passed another girl, and then another. They were running alone, like me, red and miserable. I wondered if they had left their best friends behind.

Then, far ahead, in a clump of girls, I saw Stem. I recognized their ponytails. Could I reach them? Could I beat them? I sped up again, but it was as if they knew I was coming, and they ran faster.

I couldn't go any harder—a cramp was forming in my side. I rubbed my fist against it, but it didn't help. The more I tried not to think about it, the more it hurt. I passed four girls running side by side. I looked behind me. There was no sign of Lucy, but when I faced front again, I realized the race was nearly over.

Parents and kids lined the course and clustered around the finish line. People were yelling, but I couldn't hear clearly. All I wanted to do was to pass Stem, but it was too late. I could see them, handing their numbers in at the officials' desk.

"Addy! Where's Lucy?" It was Joanne, looking worried.

"Still running. I wanted to stay with her, but she made me keep going. As soon as I get my ribbon, I'll go find her."

That seemed to make Joanne happier.

I was almost at the front of the line when Stephanie and Emma came around the other side of the rope fence and stood beside Joanne.

"We finished thirty-ninth and fortieth!" Stephanie announced proudly. Of course they had. That meant I was probably eightieth or ninetieth. But then the woman at the timing desk took my nametag with my number and stuck it on the space marked 65.

Twenty-five places behind Stem! I couldn't stop smiling.

"How did you do?" Joanne asked when I came out of the chute.

"Sixty-fifth," I said.

"That's terrific!" She turned to Stem. "Isn't that great, girls?"

Stephanie and Emma looked as if someone had forced them to drink lemon juice.

"You did great too," I said, which made them look even madder.

I didn't have to go far to find Lucy. She was already lined up for her ribbon, panting and wiping her forehead with her shirt.

Joanne, who had followed me, reached over the rope fence to hug her.

"I'm all sweaty, Mom," Lucy said, but Joanne didn't care. I'd never seen her so happy. The line moved ahead and Lucy went with it. We lost sight of her, but Joanne couldn't stop saying, "I knew you could do it!"

The next time we saw Lucy, she had her ribbon. "Here," she said, putting it into her mother's hand. "I finished one hundred fourteenth. I quit."

"What do you mean, you quit?" Joanne said. "You just said you finished one hundred fourteenth."

"I didn't mean in the race. I mean now. I quit running club. I hate it. I hate running. And all I do is slow Addy down."

I couldn't believe she was talking to her mother that way and quitting in front of Stephanie and Emma, who looked embarrassed. Maybe they were afraid Lucy was going to say they were the other reason she hated running club.

"Addy doesn't mind," Lucy said.

Doesn't mind what? I should have been paying attention.

"She'll have to run by herself," Joanne said. "Do you think that's fair?"

I didn't give Lucy a chance to answer. "It's okay," I said. "Lucy's right. I don't mind." Actually I did, *kind* of, but there were only a couple of races and a few more weeks of practice left.

"She'll do better without me anyway," Lucy said. She looked at Stephanie and Emma. They looked surprised, but I think it was because Stephanie's father had just showed up to drive them home. Usually it was her mother.

Once they were gone, Joanne said, "We're not done discussing this yet. We'll talk more at home."

"Okay," Lucy said, but from the way she said it, I had a feeling that for the first time Joanne might not get what she wanted.

Chapter 15

That night I dreamed I lost my hearing aids and forgot my runners the morning of the next race. I was late to the starting line and couldn't hear the starting gun. I had to run barefoot. All the other girls were wearing platform shoes. I had to hop around to avoid having my feet crushed. I woke up before the race ended.

Mom took me to the audiologist before school. My hearing aids were fixed. At least that part of the dream wouldn't come true. But the audiology clinic was so crowded, I didn't get to school until recess. Lucy was hanging out by the monkey bars.

"Guess who has to take swimming lessons?" she said.

"But you know how to swim."

"My mother said if I quit running club, I have to do something."

"Maybe you should come back."

Lucy shook her head. "I like swimming. Maybe we can take lessons together!"

"I have to take private," I reminded her. My mother doesn't believe I can hear the teacher without my hearing aids.

"We can take private lessons together," she said. "Anything is better than running. But I'll come watch you race. I want to be there when you beat Stephanie and Emma!"

"Don't say that!"

"Why? They didn't hear."

"You'll jinx it," I said.

At the first practice after Lucy quit, Kelsey said, "Stephanie and Emma think they're better than you, but you can beat them. Our sister said so too."

They were being nice, but I wished people would stop saying I was a good runner. I'd only been in three races. What if sixteenth place was beginner's luck?

I was faster than Kelsey and Miranda though—fast enough that I couldn't run with them during practice. So I ran alone until I caught up to Miss Fielding.

She was telling Stephanie and Emma how she used to run with the Canadian cross-country team and compete all over the world. Stephanie and Emma gave each other knowing looks, like they were going to make the Canadian team some day too.

"You ought to consider joining the Tornadoes, Addy," Miss Fielding said. She turned toward Stephanie and Emma. "Aren't you girls in that club?"

From the length of time it took to answer, you'd think she'd asked them what they ate for lunch the fourth day of grade two. Finally they mumbled something. Then they sped off as if they'd heard a starting gun.

"Not too far ahead, girls," Miss Fielding called after them. She looked at me. "It's better to keep a steady pace, like you're doing."

"I don't think I'll join a running club," I said. "I don't know anyone in one."

Miss Fielding nodded toward Stephanie and Emma. "What about them?"

"We're not really friends."

"Well, you've definitely got a gift for running," Miss Fielding said. "You should keep it up."

During science class, we had to show Mrs. Shewchuk our sketches and a list of supplies. When she saw *dead hearing-aid batteries* on our list, she looked confused.

"For stars," I explained.

"That's a good idea," Mrs. Shewchuk said. "Very inventive!"

"Addy wants to use tuna cans because we're doing Pisces," Sierra said.

"No, I don't," I said.

"You did," Sierra said.

"Last week. Not anymore."

Mrs. Shewchuk acted as if she hadn't heard. "Can you think of a recycled item that looks like a fish?"

I looked at the floor to keep from getting angrier. "Soles from shoes?" I said.

"That's creative," Mrs. Shewchuk said. "With a bit of paint or trim, you can easily turn a sole into a sole." She laughed at her own joke and moved on to Stephanie and Henry, who had been arguing about whether to use toy guns in their mobile of Orion the hunter.

"I thought we were going to use pie plates for fish," Sierra said.

"I thought we were going to use them for stars."

"No, we're using your hearing-aid batteries." The way she said it, you'd think I wore the hearing aids to make her jealous.

"We're using yours too," I reminded her. "And we can use pie plates for the biggest stars. If everything is the same size, it will be boring."

"Girls, is everything all right?" Mrs. Shewchuk was standing behind me. I kept quiet. Let Sierra answer. She was the one with the problem.

"We're trying to figure out how to add balance to our mobile," Sierra explained.

"I'm sure it will be lovely," Mrs. Shewchuk said.

"You don't know how lucky you are," Sierra said after Mrs. Shewchuk had walked away.

I didn't understand.

"Your batteries die, and all you have to do is throw them away and get new ones. I have the kind that you throw away *and* the kind you have to charge. My mother complains that they're so expensive and always says, 'You think I'm made of money!'"

"At least nobody ever asks to borrow them," I said.

"Huh?"

"In grade three, Mr. Needleman—the custodian—came into class and asked me for a battery. It was so embarrassing. Stephanie and Emma kept calling him my boyfriend."

"So what? They're mean. But hearing aids are easy. If something happens to my implant, I have to go to the hospital."

"Really? What's that like?"

"I don't know," she said. "It's never happened. But it could."

I thought, So could a stampede of unicorns down Whyte Avenue. "But you like your implant," I said.

"What made you think that? I hate it. I'm a freak."

"No, you're not. I am. I'm like somebody's grandmother. Nobody our age wears hearing aids."

"Nobody any age wears implants," Sierra said. She was about to say something else, but Mrs. Shewchuk walked by, and Sierra turned back into her I'm-more-important-than-you self.

"Do you have a hot glue gun, Mrs. Shewchuk?" she asked. "We need to attach fishing line to the batteries."

"We do?" I asked. What I really wanted to know was, *If you hate your implant, how come you're always giving speeches about it?*

But it was too late. We were done pretending we had anything more in common than a science project.

"It was so weird," I said to Lucy on the way home. "One minute she was saying how lucky I am to have hearing aids, and then Mrs. Shewchuk came by and she was Little Miss Perfect again."

"Maybe she changed the subject because she felt stupid," Lucy said.

"About what?"

"Making a big deal about how her implant is great and costs so much when, really, she hates it. Maybe she's afraid you'll tell everyone. Maybe people made fun of her at her last school. Maybe that's why she moved."

Sometimes Lucy's imagination runs away with her.

"Okay, maybe that's not it," Lucy said. "But don't you think it's kind of interesting that you thought she thought implants were cool, and it turns out she'd rather have hearing aids?"

"She didn't say she'd rather have hearing aids. She said I'm lucky I do. But all I want is to be able to hear like you do. Like a normal person."

Lucy was quiet. If only having normal hearing was as easy as saying, "I quit."

Chapter 16

The morning of the next race, I was emptying my backpack at my cubby when Henry pointed to my FM. "Do you use that at night?"

"No," I said. Why did he care what I used at night?

"Can I borrow it? For my radio club? We're meeting tomorrow. I bet it has really cool electronics."

"Um, no," I said. Did he think it was a show-and-tell toy?

"I'll take good care of it. I promise."

Sierra walked up behind us. "You can borrow mine, Henry," she said. "I'll come with you. I can answer any questions."

"Really?" he said. "That would be so cool."

I had to walk away before I said, *You hate your implant, but you want to talk about your* FM *to a bunch of radio club geeks?*

"Did you hear that?" I asked Lucy as we waited for Mrs. Shewchuk to take attendance.

"You mean Sierra offering to go to Henry's electronics club?"

"Yeah. What's wrong with her?"

"She likes attention," Lucy said.

"Then she should like her implant. Look at all the attention she gets from it."

"That's because she talks about it all the time," Lucy said. "If she acts like she likes it, people think she's important. If she says she hates it, they feel sorry for her."

I hadn't thought about it that way. And it was exactly what made me not like her. Also the way she acted as if she was an expert on everything.

But Sierra did know some things. She took the soles Mrs. Shewchuk brought us that morning and began snipping until they looked more like fish than shoe parts.

"Here," she said and handed me a black Sharpie marker. "Watch me, and do what I do." She drew spots and lines and *voila!* A fish!

"You're really good," I said.

"I know."

I would have just said thank you. But as my grand-mother says, it takes all kinds.

We spent the rest of the period finishing the mobile. It looked way better than I'd expected. Everyone's did. Sarah and Lucy's had musical notes, and Ursa Major was made from bent paper clips. Stephanie had convinced Henry not to use guns, so their mobile had bows and arrows made from tooth-brushes, twigs and fishing line.

Next week we would present oral reports. Naturally Sierra wanted to read ours, but Mrs. Shewchuk said we had to take turns.

"These are paired projects, and I want to hear from everyone," she said. "You all have something important to say."

The race that day was back at Laurier Park. Because we'd already been there, we didn't have to go over the course, but Miss Fielding did a walk-through anyway. "It's a good way to warm up," she said.

"Besides, not everybody's been on the whole course," Emma said, smirking.

"Emma, did you say something?" Miss Fielding asked.

"Just that it's a good idea," she said.

I don't think Miss Fielding believed her, but what was she supposed to do? Call her a liar? That's when I remembered Joanne's advice about using anger to fuel adrenaline.

Should I thank Emma? The thought made me laugh.

"What's so funny?" Stephanie demanded.

I smiled but didn't answer.

"Come along, girls." Miss Fielding waved us toward her. "Let's do this so I can get you to the starting line. I don't want you in back again."

Kelsey and Miranda babbled during the entire walk-through. They talked about their oral reports and dance recitals and whether 3D-TV was better than hi-def. After they couldn't agree whether Taylor Swift should get a tattoo, I said I had to turn off my hearing aids to save the batteries.

"Oh, of course," Miranda said, as if I'd said something important, which, I guess, to her it was. But it was more polite than saying, "I have to turn them off because listening to you is killing my brain cells."

When we got to the starting line, Miss Fielding lined us up, as she had the first day. But this time she put me in front with Stephanie and Emma. After Miss Fielding left, I moved away from Stem. Some girls from the second row came forward and filled the space.

I bent over and stretched, then jogged in place like the girls on either side of me. They were all talking to each other. I switched off my hearing aids. I didn't want to listen to anyone. I saw the Adidas man raise his gun, so even if I didn't hear it, I would see him pull the trigger and know to run.

The gun was so loud I had no trouble hearing it. The entire first row of girls surged forward together across the grassy field. I remembered what Miss Fielding had said at practice: "Keep some girls in front of you. Let them set the pace. You're strong enough to overtake them if you keep them within fifteen meters."

Within seconds, nearly thirty girls were ahead of me. I sped up and passed the ones blocking my view of Stem. We were separated by a group from Barton Elementary. I liked their purple T-shirts, but not how slowly they were running. I passed them too, careful to stay far enough behind Stem so they wouldn't see me.

I felt like I was playing a spy game, not running in a race. It was fun. Or maybe it was the running that was fun. I didn't have a cramp. I wasn't out of breath. The field had narrowed slightly into more of a path. Everything felt good. Everything was working. Except it was so quiet. It was a little weird, so I reached up and turned on my hearing aids. I could hear feet pounding on the grass. I knew there were girls behind me. I kept waiting for the sound of someone about to pass me. That made me nervous, so I turned my hearing aids off. Now it was peaceful again.

I was halfway through the course. I could tell because we were passing the path to the boat launch. Last summer one of my dad's co-workers took us out on the river from here. We had never been on a boat, and my mother wanted me to take off my hearing aids in case we tipped over.

My father said that was ridiculous. "Cruise ships would go out of business if you couldn't wear hearing aids on a boat!" he said. That didn't make me feel better, but at least my mother stopped nagging me. I wore my hearing aids, and everything was fine.

The path narrowed to about the width of a sidewalk. I could still see all the girls in front of me. The one who had been leading since the beginning—a tall, thin girl with a school shirt I couldn't read from this far back—was about to be passed by a curly-haired girl in a green and yellow shirt.

I sped up. That's when I realized I was right behind Stem. I started to pass them, but when they saw me, they sped up. I tried to pass them again, and they sped up again. Then they spread out so I couldn't go around or between them.

I knew I could run faster, but it didn't make a difference if they wouldn't let me pass. Then I felt something behind me. When I looked back, I saw a bunch of girls. I switched on my hearing aids in time to hear them yell at Stem to get out of the way. When Stem finally moved over, we all ran past them.

"What idiots," a short girl said.

"What school are they from?" another asked.

"Mackenzie, like her," the short girl said, looking at me.

"I don't like them either," I said and switched my hearing aids back off. I didn't want to hear more, and I didn't want to talk. Actually, I kind of wanted to yell, *I passed you! How do you like that, Stem!?* But more than that, I wanted to run as fast as I could. Maybe I wouldn't finish in the top ten, but if I could stay ahead of Stem until I crossed the finish line, that would be as good as winning.

The rest of the race went by quickly. I was sweating harder than I had in the other three races combined. As we neared the finish line, I turned my hearing aids back on.

I had never seen my mother so excited. "Addy! Addy! You finished sixth!" she yelled.

I had done it! I'd finished in the top ten! And beaten Stem!

My mother held out my water bottle. I handed my hearing aids to Lucy. After I emptied the bottle over my head, I dried my ears with the bottom of my shirt and put my hearing aids back in.

I was so happy I almost hugged the lady at the official's table as she handed me a purple ribbon and a blue form. I was reading the form—a running club application—when I felt a tap on my shoulder. I turned, expecting to see my mother, but it was the short girl who had called Stem idiots. She was holding an orange ribbon that said seventh place.

"I'm Catherine," she said. "Was this your first race?"

"My fourth." I showed her my ribbon. "I'm Addy."

"That's great," she said. "Especially after what those girls did. They go to your school, right?"

I nodded. "They didn't want me to beat them."

"So they blocked everyone?" She shook her head, then looked at the form. "Are you going to join?"

"I don't know," I said. "Are you?"

"I'm already in it. It's a great club."

"The Tornadoes?"

"No—the Road Runners. The Tornadoes stink."

I thought about telling Catherine that Stem ran with the Tornadoes, but she was still talking. "The best runners are Road Runners. Like Nina." She pointed to a curly-haired girl with a medal around her neck. It was the girl with the green and yellow T-shirt. "She wins every week. And Kristine and Maddison—they're always in the top five."

Lucy came running over, breathless. "They did worse than last week! Fifty-fourth and fifty-fifth!"

"Who?" Catherine asked.

"The girls who blocked the path," I explained.

"They blocked the path?" Lucy's eyes widened.

Catherine and I nodded. While we were telling Lucy what happened, Catherine's mother and mine found us. They introduced themselves to each other. I heard my mother saying, "Yes, those are hearing aids. She's worn them since she was three."

She started telling Catherine's mother "The Story." I wondered if Sierra's mother had a story she told everyone about Sierra's cochlear implant. But Sierra probably wouldn't mind. She talked about her implant all the time. It made her feel important, like she was the star of her own hearing-loss story.

I wanted to be the star of a different kind of story.

On the way home, Mom and Lucy couldn't stop talking about the race and my superstar future as a cross-country runner. All I could think about was Mrs. Shewchuk saying, "Everyone has something important to say." Sierra thought she was the only one who had something important to say. She was wrong.

I pictured Lucy, standing up for herself and telling her mother, "I quit," in front of everyone.

If Lucy could do it, so could I—although not in front of everyone. I waited until after my mom dropped Lucy off. As we drove toward home, I said, "Please stop talking to people about my hearing aids."

She looked confused. "When did I do that?"

"All the time. And just now, with Catherine's mother."

I expected her to argue, but instead she said, "She asked," in a hurt kind of voice.

"So just tell her I wear them. You don't have to tell the whole story. If you want to talk about me, say I'm a good student. Or a good runner."

My mother didn't answer. She looked as if she was trying to remember something. When she finally spoke, she sounded a little sad. "I'm so used to speaking up for you, I forget you have your own voice." She smiled, a small smile. "You're growing up."

I was still holding the Road Runners form. "I think I'll join," I said. "It might be fun."

After dinner I filled out the application form. There was a space for medical conditions, such as asthma or allergies. I checked "none." Then I handed it to my mother so she could sign the parent or guardian line.

She studied the application carefully. I was sure she would write *hard of hearing* on the medical conditions line. I got ready to say, "My hearing has nothing to do with running." But she left the line blank.

"I am going to tell everyone you're my champion Road Runner," she said.

Then she signed her name and handed me back the form.

Author's Note

Whenever I read a story, I wonder how much is true and how much the writer made up. In case you're that kind of reader, here's the scoop. Most of this story is made up. The significant true details are that my daughter Elizabeth joined her school running club when she was in elementary school (but not to keep anyone company), she has worn hearing aids since she was three (but nobody teased her about them), and Jim Ryun is a champion distance runner who lost his hearing when he was four years old and gained a lot of confidence when he discovered he had a gift for running.

Addy is no expert on cochlear implants, so her statement that Sierra had to get her head cut open isn't exactly accurate. If you're interested in learning more about implants, there's lots of information on the Internet.

Acknowledgments

A lot of people helped bring Addy to life, and I hope my memory isn't failing as I attempt to remember them all.

For the initial encouragement that gave me the confidence to move the story out of my head and onto paper, I am grateful to Maggie de Vries. For prodding, cheerleading and astute feedback, I thank Caterina Edwards, Mar'ce Merrell, June Smith-Jeffries, Lorie White, Lorna Schultz-Nicholson, Holly Robinson, Stewart O'Nan, Therese Gaetz and Dawn Ius. For feedback on hearing loss, I thank Candy Carrier and Emily Bennett. For providing me with young readers' perspectives, I thank Sarah Bacon, Odessa Bauer and Jaren Wiley Voigt.

Tony Abbott's novel, *Firegirl*, inspired me. Tony himself was very helpful when I turned to him for advice about trimming the final version of Addy. I am also grateful to Jim and Anne Ryun, for sharing stories of what it was like for Jim to grow up with hearing loss and how it indirectly led to his running career.

The folks at Orca have been wonderful to me, especially Sarah Harvey, whose enthusiasm pulled me out of my malaise, and Christi Howes, the best editor I've never met.

I am particularly grateful to the Alberta Foundation for the Arts, whose funding gave me the freedom to devote the time I needed to revise and polish *Addy's Race*.

Finally, I want to thank my family: Elizabeth, for turning off her hearing aids during an elementary school race; Noah, who kept asking when I was going to finish the story already; and David, who encourages me in so many ways, not the least of which is by insisting it's okay if we have take-out or frozen food for dinner every night.

Debby Waldman is the co-author of *Your Child's Hearing Loss: A Guide for Parents* (Plural Publishing), which she began writing after learning that her then three-year-old daughter would need to wear hearing aids for the rest of her life. *Addy's Race* is inspired by her daughter and the many children she learned about while working on the book. Debby is also the author of the Orca picturebooks *A Sack Full of Feathers, Clever Rachel* and, with Rita Feutl, *Room Enough for Daisy.* She lives in Edmonton, Alberta, with her husband, daughter and son.

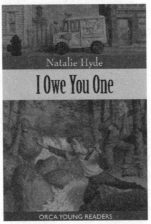

Natalie Hyde

I Owe You One

ORCA YOUNG READERS

9781554694143 $7.95 pb

According to his best friend Zach, Wes owes a life debt to the old lady who saved his life. Wes isn't sure that Zach is right, but it doesn't help that Wes keeps hearing his dead father's voice saying things like, *A man pays his debts, Wes*, and, *A man always treats a woman with respect, Wes*. But how does a guy go about paying back a life debt anyway? And what if it involves a transmission tower, an ice-cream truck and a few sticks of dynamite?